The Kissing Skunks

The Kissing Skunks

By Gloria Deák

Illustrated by Cheryl Nathan

STAR BRIGHT BOOKS

NEW YORK

Published in the United States of America by Star Bright Books, Inc., New York.
The name Star Bright Books and the Star Bright Books logo are registered trademarks of Star Bright Books, Inc. Please visit www.starbrightbooks.com.

ISBN-13: 978-1-932065-46-6
ISBN-10: 1-932065-46-6

Printed in Thailand 9 8 7 6 5 4 3 2

Library of Congress Cataloging-in-Publication Data

Deák, Gloria.
  Kissing skunks / By Gloria Deák ; illustrated by Cheryl Nathan.
    p. cm.
  Summary: When Harriet the skunk finds the perfect white hat in an antique store and takes it home to model for her husband, he notices that her new find contains a lively surprise.
  ISBN 1-932065-46-6
  [1. Skunks--Fiction. 2. Hats--Fiction.] I. Nathan, Cheryl, 1958- ill. II. Title.

PZ7.D339237Kis 2005
[E]--dc22
                                                    2005010486

To my dearest Éva.
My firstborn, my only born, my radiant offspring.
—G.D.

For my mother, Florence, and my brother, Donald.
—C.N.

Once upon a time, there were two skunks named Harriet and Harry who loved each other very much. They were husband and wife.

They lived in the country not far from town in a house that trapped the sunlight.

One morning, Harriet woke up feeling very happy. She looked into the mirror and said, "You are beautiful. *You* ought to have a new hat."

She put the laundry bag full of dirty clothes on her head, tied the string under her chin and said, "You look pretty in that, too."

She wrapped a large towel around her head and said, "You look pretty in that."

She took her husband's red-and-white striped shirt, twisted the sleeves to make a turban, and said with a smile, "You look pretty in everything."

Harriet ran into the kitchen where Harry was making breakfast. Harry always made breakfast. He loved tossing pancakes into the air.

"Oh, Harry," she said, "I'm going into town today to buy a new hat." And she gave Harry a kiss before he could flip another pancake.

"Good idea," said Harry, kissing her right back. "What color will it be?"

"I don't know," said Harriet. "I'm not sure at all. What color do you think it should be? Should it be. . ."

yellow

Or purple

Or orange

Or green

or red or pink or blue

But before Harry could answer, Harriet said, "Maybe white. I think I would love a white hat."

Harry, who liked to wear bright colors himself, looked at Harriet and said, "Oh, yes, white. With your beautiful dark fur and your white streak you will look very special in white."

Harriet was glad he agreed. Then they smiled at each other as people who love each other very much do.

Soon after breakfast, Harriet kissed Harry goodbye and hurried into town to buy her new hat. It was Thursday. She was always free from work on Thursdays.

Harriet was a radio announcer. When she was at work, she wore ear phones. Radio listeners loved hearing her voice. She spoke so sweetly.

Luckily for Harriet, it was a fine day. It was a truly fine day for shopping.

The first shop she visited had all sorts of wonderful hats. There were green hats, red hats, blue hats, and purple hats, but there were no white hats.

The next shop had lots
of hats just as wonderful.
There were stiff straw hats,
warm fur hats, and soft wool hats.

There was even a hat with a tassel so long it was curled around a sleeping cat.

But there were no white hats.

Harriet visited shop after shop, but she could not find a white hat anywhere.

She began to feel weary and disappointed. "Perhaps this is not my day for a hat after all," she said to herself, and decided to take the bus home.

Still, she did want that new hat. And besides, Harry had so many hats and caps.

He had a fishing cap,

a baseball cap,

a bowler hat,

a Stetson,

a top hat which he
wore on special
occasions,

a straw boater
for the summer,

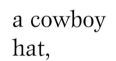

a cowboy
hat,

and a helmet
for riding his
motorcycle.

Harriet had a helmet,
too. In their helmets
and goggles, the two
skunks looked
awesome.

Harry's most favorite hat of all was
something that looked like a short
stove pipe. It had an upturned brim
and a bright band of red.

The hatter designed
that one especially
for him. It was
a Harry hat.

Designed for Harry

"Maybe someone should design a hat for me, too," thought Harriet. "No. I'd rather pick one out."

As she walked to the bus stop, a little shop caught Harriet's eye. She had never paid much attention to it before. It didn't look like a hat shop. Everything in the window looked very old. And some things were very dusty.

Right in the middle of
the window was the *most*
beautiful white hat she
had ever seen. It was
made of satin, and was
decorated with white
berries, white flowers,
white lace, white feathers,
and it had white ribbons
floating from it. Harriet
had never seen a
hat quite like that.

It was really *very special*.

She burst into the shop and pointed to the window. "I would like to try on that hat," she said.

"No, I'm sorry," said the saleslady. "Nothing can be tried on because all the things in the shop are antiques, and they are all very old."

Even though she couldn't try the hat on, Harriet decided to buy it.

It came in a very large box.

She decided that she would hide
the hat when she got home and
show it to Harry after supper.

After supper, while Harry was reading the newspaper, Harriet walked into the room wearing her beautiful new hat.

"Do you like my new hat, Harry?" she asked.

Harriet walked all the way across the room. And she walked all the way back. She wanted Harry to see the beautiful trimmings from this side and that. She was *sure* he would like it.

Harry didn't know what to say. He could see
Harriet's new hat, but he could hardly see
Harriet. He wondered how Harriet herself
could see. The hat was so big it covered her eyes.

As she walked forwards and back in front of
him, all the berries, the lace, the flowers, the
ribbons, and the feathers jiggled and wiggled
so much that Harry thought the hat was alive.
Suddenly . . . *Zoops!* It was!

A little mouse jumped out of the hat right onto
Harry's lap. Harry could not help laughing.
He laughed and laughed with his hand over his
mouth. He didn't want Harriet to hear him.
But he was shaking so much that the little
mouse became frightened and scurried away.

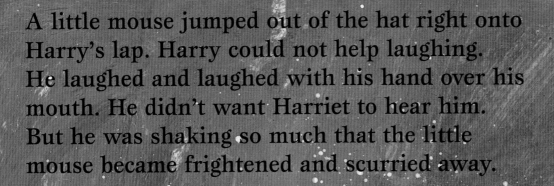

From under her beautiful hat,
Harriet peeked out at Harry.
She saw that his face was
full of smiles. She knew
that he loved her hat
as much as she did.

"I'm so happy you like
my new hat, Harry,"
she exclaimed joyfully.

"Well," said Harry,
"it's the biggest and
liveliest hat I've
ever…"

But Harriet didn't let him finish.
From somewhere under the wide
brim of her beautiful new hat, she
gave Harry a big kiss. Harry
kissed her right back.

They gave each other . . .

. . . kisses,

and saved the rest
for the next day.